Beauty and the Beast

Retold by Kay Brown
Illustrated by Gerry Embleton

There was once a merchant who, because of bad luck and greedy partners, had lost almost all his money. His wife was dead, but he had three daughters who had been used to the best of everything all their lives. One day, quite suddenly, they were told by their father to pack a few belongings as they were to move to a tiny cottage in the country.

When the girls saw their new home the two oldest – who were rather spoiled – began complaining that they could never be happy in such a poor house. The youngest daughter, however, whose kind heart and ready smile had earned her the name of Beauty, took their father's hand. Trying to comfort him, she said, "It may not be very grand, but at least here we may all stay together."

After almost a year in their new home
the merchant heard some good news: a ship
bringing goods for him to sell was due in
harbour. He decided to journey there at once!
After all those months with no luxuries or
presents you can imagine how excited the
girls were! The eldest daughter asked her
father to bring back a fine silk gown,
trimmed with lace, in a color to match her

hair. The second girl wanted a fur bonnet
from the most expensive shop in town.
Laughing, their father promised to do his
best. "But Beauty," he asked. "What shall I
bring for you?" All she really wanted was her
father's safe return, but in case she made her
sisters seem greedy by asking for nothing for
herself, Beauty said, "I miss the flowers in
our old garden: please bring me a rose."

But the merchant's good luck didn't last.
When, after travelling for two days, he
arrived at the docks he was told that the ship
had sunk in a storm and all her cargo had
been lost.

Sadly he turned for home. As night fell,
cold and exhausted, he became hopelessly
lost in a snowstorm. His horse stumbled on
against the icy wind until it seemed he could
go no further. Just as the merchant was
wondering whether he would ever see his
family again he glimpsed, through the
swirling snow, the glowing lights of a distant
castle.

It was the strangest castle he had ever seen!
Falling from his horse he stumbled up the
steps—and found the huge door open!

Although he was by now rather frightened,
Beauty's father was so tired and cold that he
forgot his fear and went inside.

He called "Hello – is anyone here?" as he walked across the great hall, but heard only the moan of the wind and the echo of his own voice. But how could the castle be deserted, he wondered, when the shadows of crackling wood-fires and lighted candles danced in every room?

At last, too weak to care, he found a warm bed and fell into it gratefully.

When he awoke early next morning he couldn't find his own threadbare clothes – but in their place was a velvet suit, fur-trimmed cloak and leather boots, all of which fitted the astonished merchant perfectly! There was a further surprise downstairs, for although dawn had not yet broken a freshly-prepared breakfast awaited him!

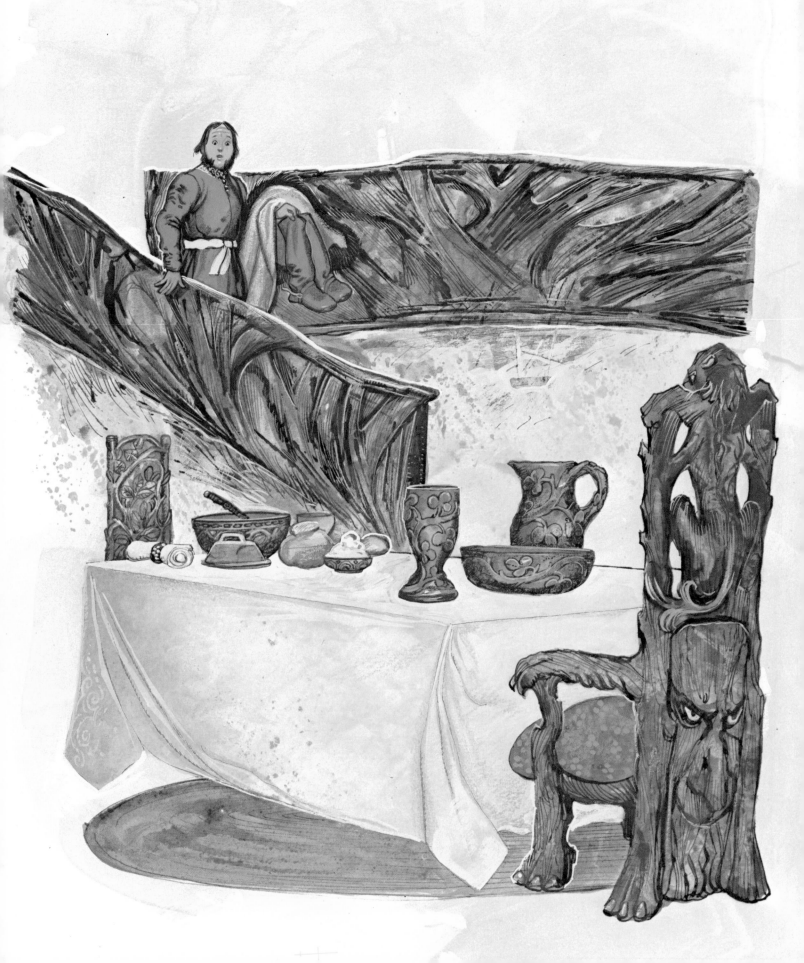

Having slept and eaten well, the merchant left the strange castle to find his horse and continue his journey. As he crossed the snow-covered garden he saw a single rose-bush in bloom and, remembering Beauty's request, plucked one of the flowers.

Instantly he heard a voice behind him roar, "Have I not given you enough, that you must steal the flowers from my garden?" He turned and was terrified to see a huge, hairy shape in a man's cloak, but with the claws and teeth of a beast!

"For your greed you must send me the first living thing which greets you on your return home!" it bellowed.

The merchant ran to his horse and rode as fast as he could until well out of sight of the castle. As he travelled he thought about the Beast's demand and hoped fervently that his dog or one of the hens might be the first creature he saw. But, as he had feared, it was Beauty who ran to welcome him, for she had been watching the lane for his return.

Miserably her father told of his bad luck in town, of finding the strange castle and of his terrible promise to the Beast. Beauty couldn't bear to see her father so troubled. She tried to appear cheerful as she packed her few possessions and said goodbye to him and her sisters, but none of them knew if they would ever meet again.

Reaching the mysterious
castle Beauty found, as her
father had, that everything
had been thought of to make
her comfortable. But there
was no sign of the Beast,
although Beauty often sensed
a lonely figure watching her
from the shadows.

One morning Beauty came
down to breakfast to find the Beast
waiting for her. She stopped on the
stairs, terrified by his strange
appearance, but he spoke in a gruff,
gentle voice. "Please Beauty, do not
be afraid. I shall never harm you."

Beauty and the Beast shared one
meal every day after that, but
although Beauty tried to talk to
him the Beast spoke very little and
kept his face turned away.

After a few weeks Beauty found
herself looking forward to their
meetings and to the rose he
remembered to leave for her
each day.

Many months passed and Beauty grew to know the huge castle and its lovely gardens. Early one misty morning, in her favorite part of the garden, she was surprised to see the Beast shuffling towards her. He knelt at her feet and asked her quietly in his rough voice, "Beauty, are you fond of me?" "Of course, dear kind Beast," she replied. "Beauty... will you marry me?" he whispered. Beauty was shocked by the sudden question, but didn't wish to hurt the gentle creature. "No," she replied. "I couldn't marry you – but I hope we may still be friends?"

The Beast said nothing; his great head hung low on his chest and he wandered slowly away.

The next day, in a magic mirror on her bedroom wall, Beauty saw her father, grey and thin, calling to her from his sick-bed. She was horrified to see how old and worried he looked; if only she could talk to him, tell him she was safe and well...

At dinner that evening Beauty begged the Beast to allow her to visit her father, promising to return as soon as he was well. The Beast sadly agreed, but gave Beauty a magic ring with which to signal her readiness to return to the castle.

Beauty awoke next morning to find herself outside her father's cottage!

The old man was overjoyed to see her again and immediately began to feel better. Even Beauty's sisters seemed glad she was safely home and they all listened in amazement to her stories of the Beast and his castle.

Beauty quickly settled down with her family again; her father's health improved every day now that his dearest daughter was home. The weeks passed happily—and Beauty forgot her promise to the Beast.

Alone once more, the sad Beast wandered through his gardens at night howling for Beauty. With each day that passed he grew more unhappy; he could neither eat nor sleep.

One evening, as Beauty prepared supper for her father and sisters, she felt the chill light of the moon through the cottage window. The magic ring which the Beast had given her seemed to flash urgently. Suddenly Beauty remembered her promise and realized she had left her kind friend to die!

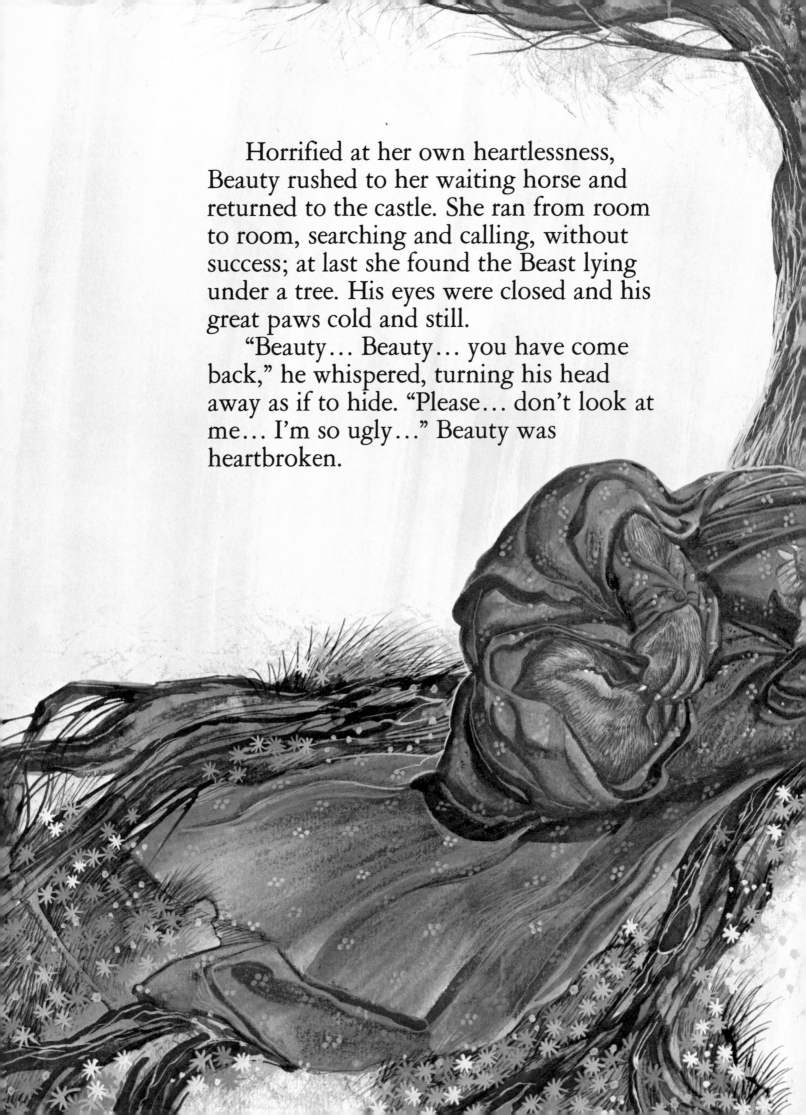

Horrified at her own heartlessness, Beauty rushed to her waiting horse and returned to the castle. She ran from room to room, searching and calling, without success; at last she found the Beast lying under a tree. His eyes were closed and his great paws cold and still.

"Beauty… Beauty… you have come back," he whispered, turning his head away as if to hide. "Please… don't look at me… I'm so ugly…" Beauty was heartbroken.

"Dear Beast," she cried, taking a paw
to warm it in her small hands. "Dear,
wonderful Beast! Please don't die—I love
you," and her tears fell onto his rough fur.

When Beauty next opened her tear-filled eyes she couldn't believe what she saw: gone were the claws and fur of the Beast, and instead her hands held those of a young man!

Smiling lovingly, he explained that a wicked fairy had long ago used her evil magic to change him from a royal prince into a beast; the spell could only be broken if a kind and honest girl came freely to love him – as Beauty had!

The very next week Beauty and her prince were married: her father and sisters came to live in the strange castle, and all lived very happily ever after.